# J. S. BACH
## THE FIRST BOOK FOR PIANISTS

### EDITED BY WILLARD A. PALMER

MW00444824

**CONTENTS**

Second Edition
Copyright © MMI by Alfred Publishing Co., Inc.
All rights reserved.  Printed in USA.
ISBN 0-7390-1464-1 (Book)
ISBN 0-7390-2236-9 (Book & CD)

*Cover art:* Johann Sebastian Bach *(1685–1750)*
   *by Elias Gottlieb Haussmann*
   *Museum der Bildenden Kuenste, Leipzig, Germany*
   *Erich Lessing/Art Resource, NY*

The selections included in this book are taken from *J. S. Bach—An Introduction to His Keyboard Music* (#638). For students and teachers who prefer an expanded introductory section and additional selections in a 64-page book, the publisher recommends the Bach introduction listed above.

All selections in this book are performed by pianist Scott Price on the CD, *J. S. Bach—The First Book for Pianists.*

The *menuet* is a dance of French origin. It is said that King Louis XIV danced the "very first" menuet, composed by Lully in 1653. Menuets were originally played at a very moderate tempo but later took on considerably more speed. They should always be played with graceful dignity.

# Menuet in D Minor

BWV Anh. 132
from the *Notebook*
*for Anna Magdalena*

# Menuet in B♭ Major

BWV Anh. 118
from the *Notebook*
*for Anna Magdalena*

Track 2

Moderato (♩ = 66–72)

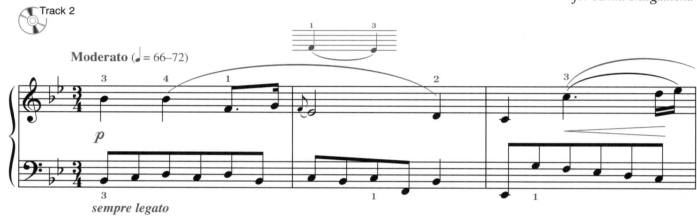

*p*

*sempre legato*

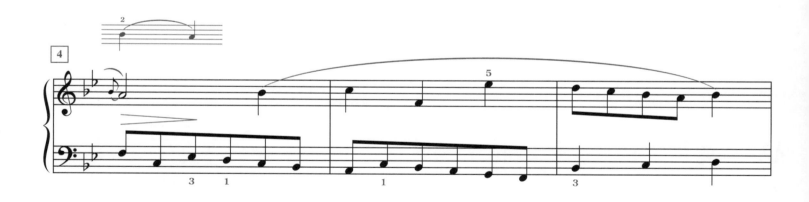

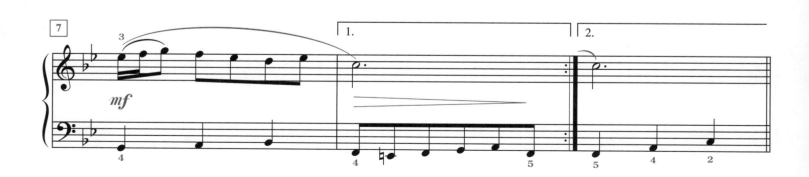

*mf*

1.

2.

# March in D Major

BWV Anh. 122
from the *Notebook*
*for Anna Magdalena*

Track 3

Moderate march tempo (♩ = 120–126)

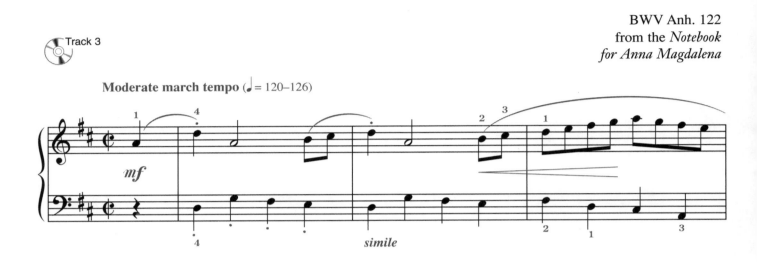

*mf*

*simile*

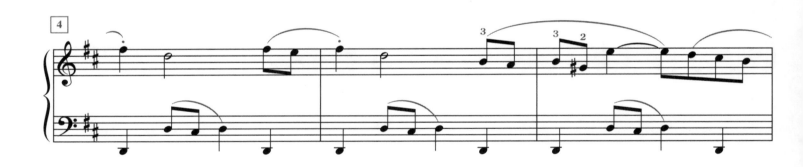

*f*

**ⓐ** This ornament combines the long appoggiatura and the trill. This is also an example of "over-dotting."
See the explanation under DOTTED RHYTHMS on page 24.

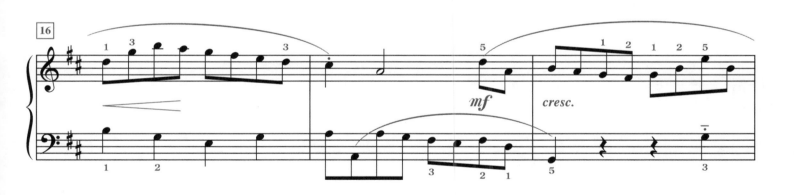

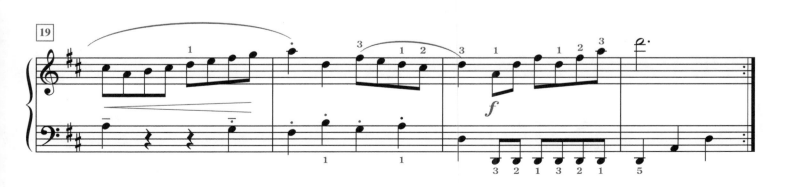

# Menuet in G Major

BWV Anh. 114
from the *Notebook*
*for Anna Magdalena*

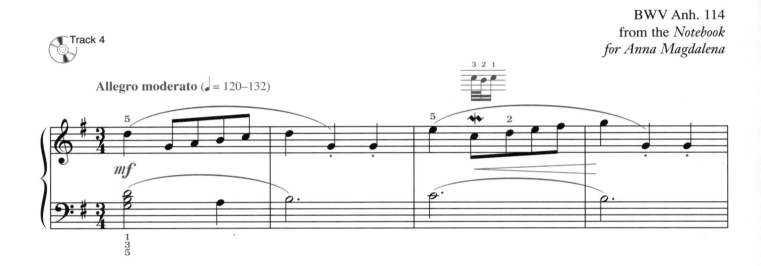

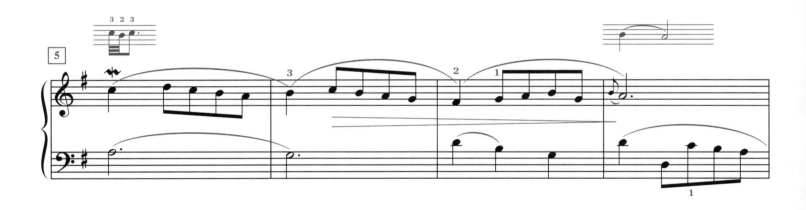

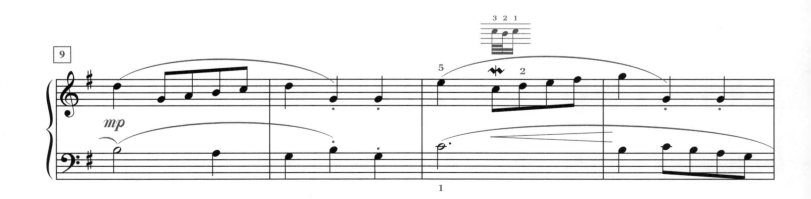

# Menuet in G Minor

BWV Anh. 115
from the *Notebook*
*for Anna Magdalena*

Track 5

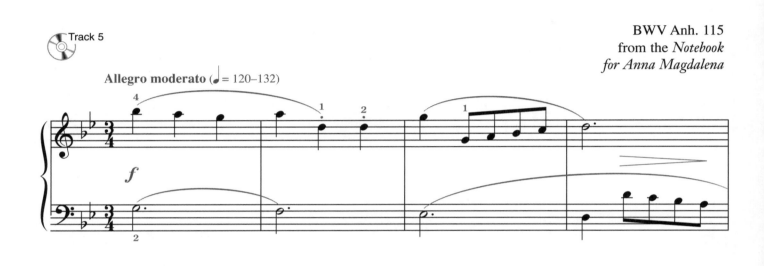

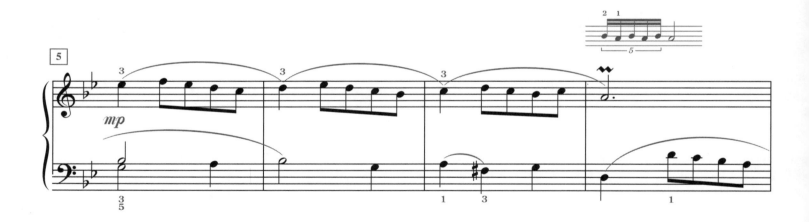

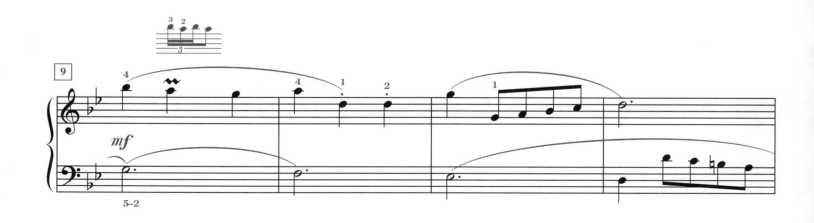

ⓐ The trill may have a termination:

A *musette* is an instrument of the bagpipe family.  Selections titled *Musette* were originally imitations of that instrument.  The melody of this selection resembles those played by the bagpipe, and the basses almost have a droning effect.  This style of bass writing, with repeated octaves, was called "murky bass."

# Musette in D Major

BWV Anh. 126
from the *Notebook*
for *Anna Magdalena*

# March in G Major

BWV Anh. 124
from the *Notebook*
for *Anna Magdalena*

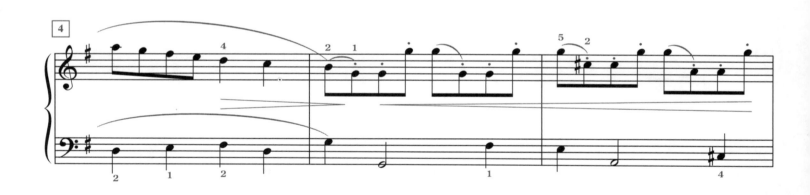

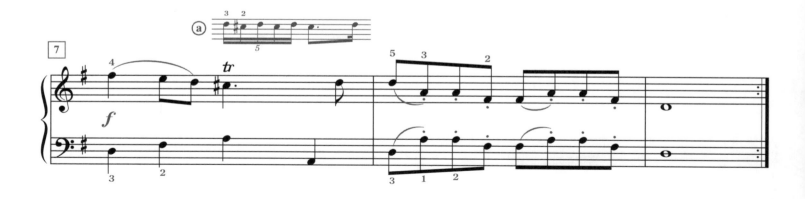

**ⓐ** This is an example of "over-dotting."  See the explanation under DOTTED RHYTHMS on page 24.

The *polonaise* is one of the national dances of Poland. It is always in moderate triple meter. It is more a promenade or processional than a dance. One of its characteristic rhythms is the figure , which is found in many of the polonaises of Chopin.

# Polonaise in G Minor

BWV Anh. 119
from the *Notebook*
*for Anna Magdalena*

ⓐ The dotted rhythm may be exaggerated here and in the fifth measure.

The first measure would be played: See DOTTED RHYTHMS on page 24.

# Musette

from *English Suite in G Minor*

Track 9

Andante (♩ = 56–66)

BWV 808

For a more accurate imitation of a musette, this piece may be played with continuous legato, with the same dynamic level throughout.

# Menuet in G Minor

BWV 842

from the *Little Clavier*
*Book for W. F. Bach*

# Prelude in C Major

BWV 939

# Prelude in G Minor

BWV 929
from the *Little Clavier*
*Book for W. F. Bach*

# Prelude in C Minor

*("Lute Prelude")*

Track 13

BWV 999

This selection is sometimes called the "Lute Prelude," because it was composed for lute. Bach may have played it on his own lute-clavecin (a harpsichord fitted with lute strings).

## About the Music

Most collections of easy Bach pieces contain simplified arrangements. Even the simplest selections from the *Notebook for Anna Magdalena* are usually furthur simplified. Ornaments are generally omitted or incorrectly notated or realized. Few editors have bothered to refer to the original manuscripts to ensure the presentation of a correct text, and even those editions known as "urtexts" are often inaccurate.

All of the pieces in this book are in their original form, unsimplified. They have been thoroughly researched from the original manuscripts. Some are manuscripts written by members of the family or by his students. In each case, all known early sources have been carefully consulted. All of the notes and ornaments in dark print are from these original sources. The indications in light gray print are editorial suggestions based on careful study of the proper performance of Bach's music.

### ORNAMENTATION

The ornaments used in this book are the trill, appoggiatura, mordent, and shleifer. The realizations in light print above or below the staffs show how to play them. The basic rules for playing Bach's ornaments are summarized below:

- The *trill*, indicated by *tr* or ᴧ, begins on the *upper auxiliary* (next higher scale tone). It must have at least four notes but may have as many as the tempo of the piece and the value of the note will allow.

The trill may end with an *anticipation* of the following note, or with a *termination* consisting of two notes (the lower auxiliary and the main note), which are played at the same speed as the trill.

- *Appoggiaturas* (♪) that appear in this book are indicated by small eighth notes. These are long appoggiaturas. They receive half the value of the following note. (If the following note is a dotted note, the appoggiatura generally receives 2/3 the value. In some cases they sound better when given only 1/3 the value of the dotted note.) Appoggiaturas should be accented and the main note played more softly.

- The *mordent* (ᴧ) is a "biting" ornament. The main note is quickly alternated with its lower auxiliary.

- The *schleifer* ( ᶺ ) is a "sliding" ornament, usually used to fill in the gap between a note and the previous one. An example of its correct performance is shown on page 2, in the 6th measure.

### DOTTED RHYTHMS

In Baroque music, dotted rhythms were sometimes expected to be played in an exaggerated fashion, lengthening the value of the dotted note and shortening the following short note proportionately:

$$ \text{♩. ♪} \; = \; \text{♩.. ♪} $$

This practice was called "over-dotting." Where over-dotting is appropriate in the pieces in this book, it is shown in the light-print realizations above the staffs.

*The Bach Family*
Portrait by Toby Rosenthal